Things That Suck

JANEEN SANDERSON

Copyright © 2018 Janeen Sanderson
All rights reserved
First Edition

NEWMAN SPRINGS PUBLISHING
320 Broad Street
Red Bank, NJ 07701

First originally published by Newman Springs Publishing 2018

ISBN 978-1-64096-488-4 (Paperback)
ISBN 978-1-64096-489-1 (Digital)

Printed in the United States of America

A huge thank you to all who added to the *Things That Suck* book; this includes all my friends, family, and coworkers over the years. To my parents, my sister, and my boyfriend, without whom I would never have made it through so many of the things that sucked. They have helped me up throughout my schooling, my career, and my life. I love you all very much!

Began: March 16, 1995
Thursday

1. Falling two steps and spraining your ankle
2. Crutches
3. Dr. Kvam's lectures
4. Robinson Memorial Hospital!
5. Getting your car an accident for the fourth time since you got in July (January was the last one; it's now March)
6. Wearing a neck brace for whip a lash
7. Having to get up at 6:00 a.m. five days a week
8. Seeing your boyfriend's face and entire body coated in blood, thinking that he's gonna die, wanting to puke, calling 911, and being at R.M. Hospital for four hours
9. Brady's Café run by Mark and the entire bathroom wall painted over in dark, burnt pea-green color
10. Sleeping alone when you haven't in months
11. Sleeping alone for months
12. Holding your head high
13. Luck
14. Not knowing what you want
15. Parking in Kent
16. Not being able to help
17. Being with someone just to hurt someone
18. Hurting said person and regretting it
19. Breaking up after a year and three months
20. Seeing the person whom you broke up with, and not being able to speak to him

21. Still loving that person
22. Red cars
23. Old letters
24. Friends who turn Born Again Christians
25. Death when you're close enough with that person that it hurts but not being close enough that you can cry
26. When worrying mothers who call at four o' clock in the morning, waking you up just because she had a bad dream
27. Getting dumped
28. Loving a woman and either not being able to tell her or knowing that if you said so, you'd get shit on
28. Godzilla
29. That ache in your throat, wanting to cry and hold it in at the same time
30. Not being able to kiss no matter how much you'd like to
31. Poetry readings without new poems
32. Brady's is for sure dying within a month
33. Seeing Joe
34. Going home with someone, knowing full well that you really don't want to be there
35. Trying to figure out a way to leave
36. #33
37. Knowing you still kinda love #33
38. Being out of cigarettes
39. Trying to call someone, and their line is busy
40. Working for and being judged by old incompetent yet powerful people, who have tired conventional, unquestioned, and unexamined so-called "morale." And who judge others on their own narrow grounds I hate that.
41. People who say deeply cutting things. You can think of a few choice shots for them, too, but you're too kind to tear into them except for when you finally get pissed enough and really let them have it in a most in uncharacteristic way.
42. Leaving out a word
43. Nightmares
44. Being in anything over your head

THINGS THAT SUCK

45. The price of a simple fucking cup of coffee
46. Broken watch bands and no extra watches to wear
47. Mothers who call every day with the same news as yesterday
48. Being poor enough to complain but not poor enough to sell plasma or your body
49. The screeching of train whistles and ambulance sirens
50. Hangnails
51. Sleeping on the couch for no particular reason, except you're lazy
52. When people don't take hints
53. Bright-orange sweatshirts that look almost hot pink
54. Really, really quiet Friday nights
55. It's the beginning of spring break, and I have to do my taxes.
56. Rent's due!
57. The Post Office!
58. Really bad recordings of really good songs
59. People who say Godzilla sucks
60. People who say they are orderly and controlled but really are too chickenshit to take a chance or two in life
61. Right handers
62. Really, really rude people
63. There's nothing to do in Kent.
64. Wishing things were the way they used to be
65. The unfairness of life at times
66. Breaking your very last cigarette
67. Bowling Green State University!
68. Bowling Green Ohio itself
69. The writing majors at BGSU
70. Not caring about the people you're fucking
71. Caring too much about people you can't have
72. Undeserving people with good karma
73. *Melrose Place*
74. Being turned down
75. Twenty-three-dollar books
76. The pressure of a deadline.
78. Procrastination

79. Forty-four days to graduation
80. Flying solo
81. Federal tax not withheld—$58.00
82. State tax not withheld—$29.99
83. Federal tax withheld—0.67
84. State tax withheld—$2.15
85. Guess to whom my next paycheck goes.
86. Red highlights when you're expecting dark brown
87. Not being able to have a cigarette while you're doing your taxes.
88. Bumping into someone from a past relationship
89. His girlfriend is staring at you evilly.
90. Really, really needing a cigarette—you're in a nonsmoking household, and you don't feel like going outside 'cause it's cold.
91. Sleep deprivation
92. Eight thirty in the morning when you're on vacation
93. When people disappointed you an eighth time
94. Selfishness
95. Infections
96. When your horoscope is right
97. Credit Card People
98. Breaks over
99. Break wasn't very good
100. Decades
101. Letters written for somebody who is thousands of miles from you
102. Doctors
103. Landlords
104. Smoking cigarette with imagining better times than now
105. Mushrooms
106. Feeling that you're getting older with no reason
107. Writing when you don't like to write
108. Wasting words at all
109. Playing in Brady's at Tuesday nights when you feel that it's going bad way
108. Trying to read something in Russian

109. Reading something in a foreign language and only knowing one other foreign language.
110. Pages that fall out from books
111. No poems in your head or on paper
112. Blood, especially lots of it
113. Cigarettes when you want to quit
114. Overdue videotapes
115. People who call early on a Saturday or Sunday morning
116. Amazing, how many times I'm probably mentioned in Joe's TTS book?
117. Paying bills
118. Closed on Sundays
120. "I don't know" as something between yes and no
121. Ash of "happy days"
122. Whether sucks!
123. Spelling *weather* wrong
124. Lesson plans
125. Tampons and the menstrual cycle in general (especially when you want to fool around too)
126. Snow in April
127. Daylight saving time and losing an hour of sleep when you went to bed at 7:00 a.m.
128. #123
129. Finding pictures of people who you don't speak to anymore
130. #125 (Gross!)
131. All-nighters
132. Sixty-two-pages portfolios
133. Going to bed at 5:30 a.m. when you have to be up at 7:00 a.m.
134. Getting up at 8:30 a.m. when you were supposed to be up at 7:00 a.m. and have to be at work by 8:30 a.m.
135. Parking in the fifteen-minute zone, getting a ticket
136. Picky teachers
137. Trying to dodge your professor because you know you're going to miss his class
138. Overdue library books
139. Not being able to sleep when you're completely exhausted!

140. Babbling in *The Things That Suck* book
141. Running into the man
142. Having to read 114 pages in a night
143. Feeling all scuzzy and yucky because you haven't taken a shower yet
144. Riding past an ex-boyfriend's house and looking to see if his car's there every time!
145. Overdue videotapes
146. Getting up at 2:10 p.m. when you are supposed to be up at 10:00 a.m.
147. Getting a failing grade on a test you could've passed if you had more time
148. White-haired old man who looks like Mark Twain (without the humor) and buzzes around on their three-wheeled machine and makes life as miserable as he can for his students
149. Wasting karma points by skipping a month in your MWF classes and then saying you had mononucleosis
150. Sleep deprivation
151. Bleeding
152. When you're walking and someone comes toward you, staring at you really hard, and you don't know why because you're pretty sure you don't know them, but you say hi anyhow. But the person just keeps staring at you and doesn't say hi back.
153. When you take up eight lines, saying something really stupid
154. Great books class
155. Feeling drunk when you wake up at nine.
156. Still feeling drunk at one
157. Not feeling drunk at six thirty
158. Forgetting for the one hundredth time to take back your library book
159. Robinson Memorial again
160. Having to pay a medical bill with no money
161. Losing about a pint of blood in one day
162. Ruining four towels, one pair of long johns, two pairs of underwear, one pillow, and one skirt

163. When you count on someone to help in an emergency and they bailout
164. Feeling like crap, being totally bored, and being stuck to the couch when it's gorgeous outside
165. Total boredom on a Friday night
166. Writing the last seventeen entries
167. Total boredom on Saturday night
168. Waiting for someone to call
169. Hearing about what your ex-boyfriend is doing
170. When a piercing doesn't work
171. Being lonely or being alone
172. Cleaning at ten thirty on a Saturday night
173. Knowing you have nothing better to do than clean on a Saturday night
174. Having a shitty weekend after you've had a shitty week
175. Pencils!
176. Being addicted to nicotine so much—you'll go out in the middle of a thunderstorm to get cigarettes
177. When you need to turn on electric light at one o'clock in the afternoon
178. When you need to turn on electric light in the darkness, and you don't know where the button is
179. Having to go to the bathroom so bad that you think your bladder is going to explode, and someone is in the bathroom
180. Teaching six classes five days a week when you're still learning and are technically still a student
181. Paying the university about $1,500 for the "privilege" of teaching
182. Missing those special moments with someone special
183. Listening to other people's special moments
184. Walking into the bathroom door at six thirty in the morning because somebody shut it
185. Finding things you lost a long time ago and have no use for now
186. Having tape all over your "unmentionable parts" and having to peel it off every time you have to pee!

187. Giving someone a second (third, fourth, fifth) chance and they still fuck up
188. Daily hassles
189. Lost friends
190. No health insurance
191. Life's little "ruts"
192. Itchy genitals
193. Trying to get over someone
194. Wearing your name tag out of the writing center
195. Forgetting your umbrella when it is raining
196. When you read something for class you didn't have to read
197. When notebooks fall apart
198. Vampires with dull teeth. Ouch!
199. Having five jobs but no money and being $4,000 in debt. Thank you, Visa, MC, and Discover.
200. Migraines that last for three fucking days
201. Pubic hair stuck in your teeth
202. A shitty tattoo, especially if it's your own
203. When your lover tastes like someone else
204. Taking the bus; riding the bus when you have to pee
205. Getting caught masturbating. Busted—"Just let me finish, honey. Then I'll unplug."
206. Being caught reading 201–205 out loud
207. Telling someone a client just heard them reading 201–205 out loud.
208. Being a regular underwear-less kind of woman and getting loaded, needing to pee, peeing, not hearing the pee-pee patter in the toilet water, and then remembering you wore underwear
209. Throwing away new underwear by disposing of them in the metal tampon receptacle at your feet. Just listen to the little door swing, wash the urine off your hands.
210. Not being able to phrase #210 because it's graphic
211. When you tell someone you care about the truth, even though it may hurt them, and another person lies about it just to save his ass

212. When people use *The Things that Suck* book to write really disgusting graphic things
213. Finally getting your shit together and then everything seems to get fucked up after one conversation
214. Nine fifteen doctor's appointments on a Wednesday morning when you normally wouldn't have to be up till ten
215. Windows that rattle every time a train goes by
216. When trains go by every ten minutes
217. Not being able to sleep and lying in bed for hours, trying to fall asleep
218. Lectures from people who just don't get it
219. Getting bitched at by someone when what happened wasn't your fault
220. People who don't have any common sense
221. Bad moods when you, for once, happen to be in good one!
222. Toilet seats that are left in the up position!
223. The downstairs neighbors and their fucking loud, obnoxious '80s music at seven forty-five in the morning
224. Cold showers
226. When you can't get everything done in a day that you were supposed to do
227. When the university makes you pay for two years of foreign language classes (over $2,000) when you know you won't remember a damn thing or even use it
228. When you've done the fucking assignment and your teacher doesn't call on you
229. Walking across campus in fifteen minutes
230. Wet shoes
231. Annoying people who sit by me in choir—Eric
232. Empty drawers that look really, really lonely for stuff
233. Wet shoes, especially when you don't have socks on
234. Toilet seats that are left in down position! Except special long-time cases.
235. Sinus

236. Being a student teacher and wondering why sometimes when you've spent four years taking stupid B.S. classes in order to prepare for this exuberating experience
237. When people take some for the credit and, therefore, make an absolute nil effort to succeed in the course
238. Not being able to get a check cashed since it came from another bank
239. Ravenna, Ohio
240. Stupid drivers when you're being a smart one
241. When people leave the toilet seat up (male) and he is in a female apartment
242. When people have the nerve to complain about toilet seats that are left in the up position and he is the visitor here
243. The thought of someone taking a special long-time case in my toilet (see #234).
244. Hemoglobin counts of 10.1
245. Stirrups on a gynecological exam table that are ice-cold
246. The other option of ice-cold stirrups being, leaving your shoes on, which look really funky on you without any pants or underwear on
247. Uncomfortable situations
248. When you really try to help someone and set aside other obligations and you feel as if you got nowhere
249. It's almost 3:00 a.m. and you have to be up by 7:15 a.m.
250. Feeling like shit and not really knowing why
251. The toilet seat thing again!
252. Getting two shots in your butt, one-half gram each
253. Fevers
254. People who take advantage of your kindness
256. Errands on your only day off
257. Deadlines
258. Having to mention the toilet seat thing
259. Bleeding over a pint of blood, hemoglobin goes down to 10.0, getting an infection, then once that's all over with, a virus which lasts for five days

THINGS THAT SUCK

260. Knowing I'm gonna have to face all my teachers tomorrow and beg them to understand
261. Fast-food diarriah
262. Not knowing how to spell
263. Let's return to the toilet seat. The thought that you're making somebody uncomfortable because of toilet seat sucks badly.
263. First, no way to solve this problem I'm too bad to have in my brain
263. Second, the thought that "toilet seat" will appear in this book again and again
264. Less than a month 'til graduation and no clue about the future
265. Unreturned phone calls
266. Stale, cheap doughnuts
267. An alarm clock going off early when you plan on hitting the snooze on the other one
268. The shower handle (cold) that you broke at 6:20 a.m. It's a bit too hot.
269. A beautiful spring morning when you have to be indoors until 3:00 p.m.
270. Getting up too late to take a shower but early enough so that you have no excuse not to make it there
271. Garbage again
272. Yeast infections
273. That little pool of water that forms around the top of the sink that you never see until you put your robe on it
274. Dead flowers in spring
275. Dirty dishes
276. Thursday meetings at 7:20 a.m.
277. Thursday, period.
278. Bad coffee, especially when the cream floats on top
279. Red pens running out of ink
280. Graduate school tapes
281. Graduation (?)
282. Filling up the *Things That Suck* book to waste time
283. Not being able to go to sleep early even if you're lying down by 10:00 p.m.

284. Having to fill out about forty interim report cards and make lesson plans on the weekends. So this is teaching.
285. When a shitty kid says to you in class (you're the teacher), "I don't have to listen to you. I've gone to this school longer. You can't tell me what to do."
286. Finding out this student is most likely selling drugs to another student in the same class where they're both A students
287. Sore throats
288. Knowing that #288 is really #289 because way back at #28, Pom put in another #28 after my #28
290. When you express interest in someone and it's mutual, and yet even after weeks of hanging and talking, you're still not sure where you stand
291. Being broke
292. Six papers, two very late the last three weeks of class
293. Those stupid stamps from the bar that never come off your hand
294. Getting there way before you she does
295. The concept of price and all that goes with it
296. No outlet
297. Memories that are much better than the present
298. Competition
299. Being left out
300. Bruising your hands playing congas
301. Missing *The Beat*
302. People who will not shut up!
303. Men who stare
304. Fevers
305. Waking up at 4:00 p.m. on a Saturday
306. This semester
306. Nightmare
308. When someone writes on the next page when there was still a line open on the last page so you write #306 twice
309. Hacking kind of coughs
310. When your back hurts so much, can't sit up straight
311. People who invite you somewhere and then forget about you

312. Ten-page papers due in two days—not even started yet
313. Those uncomfortable few moments before someone begins to tell you a problem
314. Halls cough drops your tongue is red, and your nose is still stuffy
315. Putting $5 of gas in your car on. Ultra-unleaded (about $20 and more) instead of the cheap shit
316. Staying after school (high school) on a Monday until 5:00 p.m. to see a stupid play (Spanish club)
317. Your own stubbornness
318. When someone takes care of numbers, not of words (see #308, which in real life is #307)
319. The trivial arguments in this book!
320. Misjudging people
321. Pencils without eraser
322. Quitting smoking on May 1
323. Backpacks that have zippers that come apart
324. People who use other people
325. Assignments like reading 105 pages—and you're on page 15—class is in forty-five minutes
326. The hospital bill isn't here yet.
327. Losing lighters
328. Having to use matches
329. Losing matches
330. Having to light your cigarette off the electric stove
331. Paying $1.50 for a fucking lighter
332. Feeling sad in the middle of the afternoon
333. Cloudy Kent days
334. Wishing you had someone to snuggle up with
335. Pillows don't replace people.
336. It's raining and your umbrella's in the car.
337. When only your mother understands how much you're hurting
338. A big ugly wasp who has been eyeing you up all week just waiting for his moment to sting

339. Three wisdom teeth come in without a problem, and then the relief is crushed by the fourth marauder.
340. Forgetting to put an "s" on erasers number 321
341. Waiting for your landlord
342. Tummy aches
343. The "s" in coming off the "Suck" of the *Things That Suck* book
344. Sittin' all alone at the student center
345. Warm apple juice
346. When your socks fall down inside your shoes
347. Women that break your heart
348. Really attractive men who are going out of the country to Africa soon
349. Being inside when it's nice and sunny outside
350. Coughing at the same time as your roommate
351. When your roommate, who is an English major, writes "you're" instead of "your," and she is the one who has been correcting your grammar for the past two years
352. When you're an English major and nobody lets you make grammar mistakes
353. Time
354. Having no voice literally
355. Swollen glands
356. When your students act like you never spent forty minutes five days a week instructing them over the information on a chapter test that took you an hour to make up
357. Cold tea that is supposed to be hot on a sore throat (Thank you, Denny's)
360. Neighbors who, in spite of your request for them to turn down their stupid blaring music, continue to blare it at 7:00 a.m.
361. When you have to call the landlord on said neighbors
362. When there are finally things goin' on the weekend and you should be studying!
363. "Liberal phlegm" (than you Gary Morris)
364. When you had to kiss, kiss, kiss your professor's butt so you can pass his class and graduate

THINGS THAT SUCK

365. When you park so you can pay the damn university $82, and when you get out to your car (after five minutes), you have a ticket, so you have to pay $10 to the damn university for a parking spot that you were using so you could give the fucking place money in the first place. Whew!
366. When you see your (loud) downstairs neighbor flips you off and spitefully goes by into her apartment and cranks her fucking music
367. When the chiropractor cranks up her price to $40, and if you didn't have insurance, you'd only have to pay $20
368. The insurance company hasn't paid me yet, so I'm liable for $366 of overdue monies.

James R. Young

James R Young, 51, of Beaver Falls, died Friday, March 29, 2002, in the University of Pittsburgh Medical Center in Oakland.

Born January 3, 1951, in New Brighton, he was the son of the late John Regis Young and Betty Elliott Young. He retired from the Laborers' District Council of Western Pennsylvania Local 833, New Brighton. He was a graduate of Beaver Falls High School, class of 1970, and had played on the football team for Coach Larry Bruno. He was a member of the West Mayfield Vets, Fraternal Order of Eagles Aerie 1342, New Brighton, and BPO Elks 348, Beaver Falls.

In addition to his parents, he was preceded in death by a brother, Jack O. Young, and a sister, Mary E. Bender.

Surviving are his wife: Bernadine Myers Gonezi Young; a son and daughter-in-law: James E. and Jody Young, Brighton Township; two daughters: Deanna Young and Darcy Pavick, both of Ellwood City; two stepsons; Thomas Gonezi Jr. and his wife, Michele, Center Township, and Charles Gonezi, Beaver Falls; 10 grandchildren: Tyler, Taylor, Madison, Kennedy, Bailey, Amber, Emily, Savannah, Chri, and Thomas; and two brothers and sisters-in-law: Bob and Linda Young, Apex, North Carolina, and William and Karen Young, Salem, Oregon.

Friends will be received Monday from 2:00 p.m. to 4:00 p.m. and 7:00 p.m to 9:00 p.m. in the Hill & Kunselman Funeral Home, www.hillandkunselman.com, 3801 Fourth Avenue, College Hill, Beaver Falls, where a service will be conducted Tuesday at 11:00 a.m. The Rev. Joel Garnett, pastor of the Trinity United Methodist Church, McMurray, Pennsylvania, will be in St. Mary Cemetery, Chippewa Township.

In lieu of flowers, donations may be made to UPMC in care of the Hill & Kunselman Funeral Home, 3801 Fourth Avenue, Beaver Falls, Pennsylvania 15010.

The Elks will conduct a service Monday at 8:00 p.m. in the funeral home.

369. When the fucking post office loses both your check from the insurance company and your visa bill
370. When you've lost around $288
371. Karma isn't working for you.
372. When you try to get in touch with someone for two whole weeks and you finally get them, and they say, "Can I call you back?" and they don't!
373. The lawn mower at 10:00 a.m. Saturday right outside your room
374. A cough in your chest that sounds really gross
375. When it hurts to swallow even ice cream
376. When the phone rings at 7:30 a.m. on a Saturday
377. The smell of Vicks all over you neck and chest and behind your ears. Ugh!
378. Getting to bed at 6:30 a.m. and having to be up at 7:00 a.m.
379. People who get drunk really early in the morning and progressively become more annoying
380. Thirty-something-year-olds who act like they're twelve
381. People who whine like a baby and think they're being cute
382. Hangovers
383. Chorus concerts on a Sunday afternoon
384. People who say they're going to do something with you and change their mind when a drug party comes up (after you bought them a ticket for a concert and bought them lunch)
385. When you're not fucking "cool" enough to hang with a bunch of deadhead losers
386. Looks like another fucking Saturday night at home alone and you're really pissed off
387. When you act like you're not really pissed off to the person mentioned in number 384 when inside you're fucking seething
388. People who say they give a shit about you but don't act like they do
389. Actions speak louder than words.
390. When you can't even remember the last time he did a favor for you

391. Being sick with more than one type of illness at a time (oh, I forgot mentally ill)
392. Stupid arguments that never get resolved
393. About fifteen cars in the street for a party that's not at your place, and you aren't going either!
394. Seeing someone whom you haven't seen in months, like, last time you heard from him was on the answering machine, and you never bothered calling back.
395. The second to last week of your senior year (and final one) of college
396. Wanting to say, "I'm sorry," but being too stubborn to admit you've done wrong
397. Not being able to sing to your favorite tape because you have laryngitis
398. Your new dress won't button over your chest, which is only a thirty-four or thirty-six B.
399. Gloomy Sundays
400. Lumps in the throat that won't move
401. When no matter what you said in the past about a certain something (i.e. clothes, music, people, car etc.) to someone, there was/is nothing you can do or say to make other party listen
402. When you try to say something from the bottom of your heart and the opposite party says, "Uh-huh."
403. How can cacti die?
404. Knowing you'll never be able to fly to San Diego to read the *TTS* book with Janeen Sanderson "reminiscing" (sp?) about bad days of 1995
405. Crying when you already have pink eye in the first place.
406. Somehow locating memories in inconspicuous places throughout your room
407. Listening to songs that remind you of something you can't quite put your finger on that make you nostalgic or sad anyway
408. Cultural differences when they come in the way of your friendship or relationship

409. Driving 135 miles in about five hours to Cleveland—you got lost in the city, trying to find a dinky little restaurant called The Big Egg.
410. It's 6:50 a.m., you have a week of lesson plans to complete, you need to get up at six, and you've been sick for two weeks.
411. Having to explain yourself or your actions when you see no need to do it
412. May 4, 1970, KSU
413. Being afraid of your feelings
414. When a twin bed is too big for just you
415. Hitting the snooze for forty minutes; now you're running late.
416. Dreams when you know you had them but can't remember what they're about
417. Mondays. Oh, God. Mondays.
418. Phone conversations with certain people who don't take the hint when you say how much work you have to do (like five different times)
419. These purple pens
420. Getting writing portfolios finished dedicated to AJ.
421. Three flights of stairs
422. *The Nun's Priest Tale*
423. Things that suck. This particularly sucks when you're in love with the most wonderful man ever, and because you have never had a normal relationship, you don't know how to behave. And you are so afraid of having sex because sex has always been a problem for you. And I "understand," but he doesn't like it.
424. Having to scratch out names in the TTS book
425. Piles and piles of dirty laundry
426. Losing your pen after just using it two seconds ago
427. Making really important phone calls at 8:00 a.m.
428. Forgetting your wallet
429. Getting a hacky sack in your pizza
430. Wednesday is laundry day
431. Trying not to get your hopes up
432. Having to write six papers in nine days

THINGS THAT SUCK

433. Late papers
434. One unexcused absence too many, bringing your first grade down one letter grade
435. Tests
436. The week before finals week and you haven't started to study.
437. Old men with stomachs that hang over their belts
438. You've got two days to study for five final exams
439. Praying for a miracle on your finals
440. When your ex-boyfriend comes over (after you were together on Tuesday night, after you slept with him) and tells you about a girl named Jill, who's three inches shorter than he is, with short blond hair. And he says he's been hangin' out with her, and they really hit it off. And she stayed over Thursday night (but they didn't have sex), but she left on Friday night to go across country.
441. She had more of an emotional bond with him in three days than you did in over a year.
442. When you realize you've been a prostitute all your life. You just never got any money out of it.
443. Trying to study after hearing number 440
444. People who ask if you're okay
445. People who say there's someone out there for you—you just have to find him
446. When you allow a friend to come over (because he sounds depressed) and he tries to grope you
447. He "self-disclosed" to someone else
448. Hearing that she's pretty
449. Questions that you really don't want to answer
450. When pillows have to replace people
451. Your teacher makes up lesson plans for you during your last five student teacher days and still wants you to teach. She was supposed to have taken over weeks ago.
452. #444 when you could get bitched at for *not* asking if someone is okay
453. Trying to book the cheapest possible flight to Madrid
454. No money again

456. Pencils cracked in the middle
457. When you're the one who has to fucking do everything around the house, i.e., grocery, shopping, cleaning, dishes etc.
458. People who owe you money
459. People who are fucking oblivious to everything!
460. When there is water leaking onto the table, but your roommate (who is lying right next to the table) can't lift a finger to clean it up, even after you've cleaned up how many of her messes!
461. Trying to remain calm
462. When your roommate who a tad bit stressed does not realize that although you may not have had a goddamn final to take (finals), you, too, have had just as stressful of a day and had fucking happened to fall asleep without seeing the water because you were so tired and woke up five seconds before she walked through the damn door
464. Black markers that leak.
465. Waiting (the last time) for your roommates to take out the trash because you're sick and tired of doing it but are too stubborn to succumb to her stubbornness
465. Not having money to go buy groceries and then getting fucking bitched out in a book for the dollar you owe (you already wrote the check and kept it lying on the table) and for the fact that your god forbid don't buy groceries when there's still food in the house
466. #459 when you really would like to make a nasty comment but don't
467. The fact that I was going to borrow a shirt in Neen's room, was in good mood, and then I saw the TTS book and am now in a rotten mood
468. Can I ask why we are doing this? (Oblivion? Disrespect?)
469. When your blood pressure and adrenaline suddenly rise.
470. After you've cleaned up many of her messes, let me remind you of the hair dye in the bathtub, the Hibiclens, the blood all over the bed, spider and wasp I had to kill (does this count?),

the wine bottles to the recycling dump (about 25 percent mine).
471. The fact that I'm arguing with my roommate and she isn't here
472. This argument—(!?*@) period!
473. Having to say sorry you don't feel you should have to but would rather smooth things over nicely and politely
474. When other people piss you off, too, but you never say a word because you have self-control like tranquility and don't want to start anything
475. Being uptight (an understatement in the same apartment with someone)
476. Kvam's final, "What the hell was that?"
477. Chaucer final, "I'm screwed."
478. Busting your ass all year and then having it all boil down to one lousy fucking final
479. Knowing you possess an intelligent mind and having a professor give a test that makes you look like you're brain-dead and have no right to be in college. I think they purposely make you look like an idiot to boost their own over-inflated egos. What a fucking shame, they forgot what it is like to be a student with a need to learn. God help the individual who shuns criticism in favor of emotion they will be the truly damned.
480. Ex-girlfriends come back to tell you they fooled around during the two years you were going out.
481. Love
482. Having a heart
483. The memory of love. The memory of a bonfire that could warm the world, but when you're on to me, you are cold; no memory will help you. The memory can only burn. In the minute the fire spits and says, "I love you"—*Pop*. Remember when we drove to the mountains and you almost fell asleep? The fire burned higher, ambrosia turned to gasoline. Red raced across my face, traveling around the orbit of my eye, and I held the view in disbelief. Remember the last time you

came up, and it was strange the red and the flames faded? Now's my time to change.
484. Dreary Maydays
485. Getting pulled over by the man for DWB (driving while black)486. When men wash dishes and act as if they've just run the marathon.
489. When your mother calls you a kleptomaniac, who is in an occult at four4:00 in the morning while 490. Bras
491. Cramps
492. Mail that arrives at 5:00 p.m. and it's the all junk mail.
493. Counting the days until when it's not something good you're waiting for
494. Callouses on your twenty-one-year-old feet
495. Humidity and frizzy hair.
496. The thought of AIDS
497. Litter training
498. Trying to decide what to do between five people
499. When someone starts treating you strangely and you have no idea what you did to deserve it
500. Overshooting your exit
501. Waiting for a phone call but knowing full well that you've got nothing better to do
502. Trying to figure out what to buy for your father on Father's Day
503. Big ants that won't die
504. Driving to the bank in Cleveland because you have 0.00 in your bank account and need to put $ back in without Mom and Dad finding out
505. Driving and crying at the same time
506. When you buy a bottle of wine and the girl in the convenience store said, "You must drink a lot."
507. Feeling that you have the things to say and no way to even begin to form the words
508. Sweating when all you do is lie on the couch and listen to music.

509. Going to church every stinking Sunday that you go to with your parents
510. Packing
511. Notices from the bank that say your checking account is "overdrawn"
512. Losing muscle tone because you're lazy
513. Getting up at 8:00 a.m. on a Saturday to go to a 10:00 a.m. appointment, a two-hour graduation (high school) ceremony
514. Lying to your mom when she finds men's socks in your laundry basket
515. When other people are in bad mood and act as if you should be too
516. All the things you have to take care of when you move
517. People who come over and take things without asking
518. Broken answering machines
519. Four days of the shits
520. Uneven sideburns
521. Foreign women
522. Having a booger you can't reach
523. Loving someone who doesn't love you back
524. Having an itch on the inside of your throat
525. Being uncontrollably dizzy
526. Getting drunk without drinking
527. Spring or summer allergies
528. The smell of campfire smoke all over your hair and clothes for days
529. When the call waiting beep goes off and you're in a deep conversation or are trying to be polite and you can't figure out who was trying to call because they don't call back
530. When you have to get up fairly early and it's getting light out as you go to sleep
531. People who have major trouble getting out of bed on their own free will (you're already up)
532. Expecting important things in the mail and not having a clue when they're supposed to arrive

533. Wanting to be in another country so bad you can taste it, knowing it's impossible (Mexico)
534. Dreams you know you have but can't recall any detail of
535. Dangling participles
536. Short fingernails that break
537. Sitting down at a piano when you haven't seriously played in about five years
538. When something incredible is going to happen in a few weeks but you can't even look forward to it because something else is worrying you too much
539. Missing kittens that you know are hiding in you apartment, just dying to freak you out
540. Leaving
541. Goodbyes
542. Waiting
543. Showerheads with no water pressure
544. Bare white walls
545. Wasting paper with five-line poems
546. Being sensitive
547. Being too emotional
548. Going home for four days
549. When you're inside and the landlord spends all day mowing the grass
550. What does distance do to communication?
551. When your sister makes you feel like a total idiot in front of her three friends and you feel silently juvenile you want to die
552. Meeting guys in laundry places who are twenty-five but you say you're eighteen, and he begins to talk to you like you're his little long-lost sister.
553. Deodorant balls
554. To leave Kathy
555. When you go to write something in the TTS book and you read #554 and realize what you were going to write isn't all that bad anymore
556. Complete exhaustion
557. To have Konnie leave, not knowing if you'll ever see him again

558. When a train suddenly leaves and you have absolutely no opportunity to say goodbye officially
559. Sobbing when you feel you can't stop
560. Hearing his voice in your head
561. When people appreciate things after they happened
562. When I don't know anything
563. A
564. When you just don't value your life much anymore.
565. When you read #563, A, you have no idea what it says, and so you ask the writer of #563. And she says she forgot what she was going to say.
566. When your shirts still smell like him
567. Getting accepted as a graduate assistant on the same day your boyfriend leaves (left)
568. UPS trucks at the house next door
569. Expecting phone calls
570. First job interviews
571. The persistence of memory (Dali)
572. Pieces of hair you cut off from someone else's head that come apart and fall all over your bed
573. Mascara that runs
574. Sleeping five hours in two days and being wide awake when you know you shouldn't be
575. Not being excited about going to Belgium and Spain because you feel other things are weighing down on your shoulders too strongly
576. Trying to say something to help, but your sarcasm gets in the way
577. Trying to say goodbye to everyone
578. Not knowing how to say goodbye
579. Pain in places where pleasure should occur
580. Smoker's hack
581. Typing a "philosophy of education" on the morning of your job interview
582. When your boyfriend tells you (while calling from a pay phone on the street), "You're too nostalgic."

583. When men can't deal with your sadness or their own
584. Having one day to pack nine months of apartment life
585. Waking up alone but feeling someone next to you and hearing him say, "Where are you going? Come over here and kiss me."
586. Ghosts
587. Clear nail polish
588. Having no appetite
589. Imitating accents
590. Trying to decide whether or not to live in the apartment across the hall (alone) from your old apartment when your roommate won't be here anymore
591. Getting drunk off one beer because you can't eat
592. Getting your period about four days early and having cramps
593. Being completely alone
594. When you realize you don't really need or want to talk to the guy you almost killed yourself for because he's too far way and he hurt you three years ago. And then you wonder if the same thing could happen with the man you truly love right now.
595. One hour developing when you just finished a roll of film today, and people in the pictures won't see each other for a very long time if ever.
596. When the principal interviewing you says (in a sarcastic way) that something on your resumé is cute
597. Missing an exit on the way back to Kent
598. The question, "Where are you now?"
599. When your mother thinks Kostia was a "friend" and keeps telling you, "Next time, find a guy that will stay around."
600. Not being able to see the TTS book anymore
601. Just realizing how much you're gonna miss Orchard Street, apartment number three
602. Feeling like you'll never be happy again
603. When your boyfriend starts crying on the phone
604. Leaving Kent for good
605. Starting a new job in a technical field and you're a creative person

606. Knowing that you have to get up at 5:00 a.m., get home at 6:00 p.m., and spend the time in between doing things at work you don't really like for quite a long time
607. Figuring out car loans
608. When you really have to take a shit but don't want anybody to hear, and you're in a public place
609. Being squished in the back of a car magna and the top down in the middle of a thunderstorm
610. Trying to find your friends at a dead show, and there are thousands of people there
611. The bickering that goes on between parental units
612. When you realize your new job is taking total control over your life
613. When the people at the top don't communicate
614. When you start a new job and all the intelligence you've collected over the years suddenly oozes out your ears on the first day
615. When it's still oozing on the fifth day
616. When your kitten takes a piss on you
617. Mondays
618. Hitting a traffic jam on the way to work at 7:35 a.m.
619. Merge left
620. The little critters that try to cross the road and then get squished by nasty industrialized motor machines
621. When the little critter isn't quite dead yet
622. Merge right
623. Those little pink memo pads that say, "While you were out."
624. Lots and lots of laundry
625. Noticing that #522 is really disgusting
626. Warmed over pasta
627. Boredom
628. Shopping malls
629. When you try to buy Camel lights box and you get home later and pull out Camel lights 100s softback
630. Smoking Camel lights 100s
631. When something big is going on but no one tells you anything

632. People who don't return phone calls
633. Long-distance calls
634. Telephones
635. Saying, "Good morning/afternoon, Andrews Industrial Controls, how may I help you?" every time you answer the phone
636. When you open a new checking account, put 1,000 in cash, and then they tell you you can't write checks for ten days, and you can't get a bank card for thirty days. Now you have no cash and no way of getting any out. And your bills are late, so you can't use your credit cards. And you can't write a check out to cash either because it closes before you can get your ass home after work in time.
637. When your cat takes a shit all over the place
638. When you have no one to complain to except this book
639. Ninety-four degrees Fahrenheit
640. Contacts that stick to your eyes
641. Bills
642. $10 occupational tax!
643. #639, especially when you know it's going to be even hotter tomorrow
644. Power outages
645. Having stuff stuck between your teeth
646. The dandruff stuff that comes off manila envelopes
647. Whoever came up with the name *manila* for an envelope?
648. When you get the batteries stuck in the radio
649. Wednesday
650. Getting barbecue sauce in tiny little cuts on the tips of your fingers
651. When you answer the phone so much your ear hurts
652. Printers
653. Bad hair days
654. Merge left
655. Dubell leach septic systems
656. Backhoe operators that can't identify a Dubell leach septic system

657. Little happy days
658. Absolutely no privacy anywhere
659. When your toilet fills up with mucky water and you think it's the septic system backing up when it's actually only air in the pipes, and you get so flipped out that you call your father who is vacationing in Canada
660. When the "y" in actually is falling off the line in number 659
661. When people drop the loop in their "y" so far down that you can't write on the next line down
662. When you're on the phone with someone and he is asking what the hell is going on, and someone else is trying to tell you, and everyone is talking at once
663. My first customer's phone call
664. Being the middle man!
665. Bad car days
666. When your car has no muffler and is loud as shit
667. The #666
668. When you can't tell your left from your right
669. People who just assume that you pay for everything
670. When the following things are broken on your car: exhaust system, one windshield wiper, transmission fluid container, the seat belt sensor, suspension
671. Driving seven and one-half hours in one weekend
672. The slave labor in India
673. Tattoo artists who are on speed
674. Getting your period two weeks early
675. When you get a really good buzz going and you burn yourself with your cigarette and lose your buzz
676. A Tupperware container that had chili in it that has been sitting in your car all weekend
677. LOS (lack of sleep)
678. Leaving hundreds of messages for people who never call back
679. Trying to get everything done during lunch hour
680. Trying to write while you bounce along PA roads
681. Mighty Whitey

682. Trying to suck down that last cigarette before going back to work
683. When your mailman is stupid
684. The dishwasher
685. Foodland doesn't open 'til eight, and I'm thirsty at seven forty.
686. When you get the urge to call your ex-boyfriend
687. Calling your ex-boyfriend
688. When a fly lands smack dab in the middle of your peanut butter parfait ice cream and drowns in the melted part
689. Finding a lump on your kitten's belly
690. That stupid fax machine
691. Quotes
692. Being put on hold
693. When five seems five years away on Friday!
694. Working two jobs
695. Not being allowed to smoke at work
696. Labels
697. Having nothing to do!
698. People get in line, and their brains fall out.
699. Trying to fill the empty spaces of work time with meaningless busy work dribble
700. When your intelligence is still oozing on the thirty-ninth day (refer to #614)
701. Used car salesmen who seem to think that they are "part and particle of God"
702. Really rude men who let the door close in your face
703. Being extremely unhappy in work life (your social life doesn't exactly thrill you either)
704. Insomnia
705. Jerry Garcia is dead on August 9, 1995
706. Hung Gu
707. Coworkers who work you into the ground
708. Ninety-six degrees Fahrenheit
709. Arguing with your parents
710. People who ask you one thousand questions in the morning
711. Ninety-eight degrees Fahrenheit

THINGS THAT SUCK

712. Hurricane Felix
713. Friday is two more days away
714. When the song "Tempted by the Fruit Another" is stuck in your head
715. The copier machine
716. When the copier repairman is really hot-looking but dumb as nails
717. When everything you touch, breaks, drop, bangs, splatters, etc.
718. When people push your buttons when you're really annoyed
719. Still oozing on the forty-sixth day (refer to #700 and 614)
720. When you're so tense, your whole perception changes
721. Not knowing exactly why you are so tense
722. It's not Friday at 5:01.
723. When you just don't measure up
724. People with really annoying laughs
725. Old men who sing show tunes
726. People who tell you to do one thing and then change their minds
727. Paul's Katherine Hepburn's impression
728. Dreaming about the one you miss
729. Moving rocks that weigh two-thirds your weight
730. Workers who can't understand some of the basic concepts of levers
731. Catching a 101-something-pound rock with your hand
732. Being trapped with your hand under a hundred-pound rock with no leverage
733. Having your hours cut again
734. Not knowing what to do
735. Hoping for success but fearing failure
736. Feeling you're standing still
737. Having to write a letter to total strangers, exposing your most embarrassing flaw
738. Watching the sunset on an empty day
739. Watching it rise again

740. Waiting for a letter that says, "I can try to finish something and should have finished five or six years ago."
750. Realizing that even though you are still much best friends with your ex-roommate and best friend, you have now officially ceased to exist in each other's "everyday worlds"
751. Flipping to the new TTS and seeing something really sad that someone had written for you
752. E-mail when it doesn't work how it's supposed to
753. When your new roommate doesn't and can't ever measure up to your old one, so you already have it in for (your new one)
754. When your best friend and her boyfriend are in your living room and you're not sure if it's a good idea to mention to one of them that you were gonna sleep on the couch because you're afraid to enter the room
755. Feeling like a third wheel
756. The above when you think, *Well, now it's my turn.*
757. Instant karma
758. Nosy people whom you've just met
759. Black cat hairs on your white pillowcase
760. Stomachaches when you're curled in the fetal position because it hurts so bad, but it doesn't help, and finally you fell asleep and then you wake up and your legs are numb
761. Kitty litters at the bottom of the toilet. Why?
762. Spending too much $ on alcohol
763. When you get an e-mail letter from Moscow and it says, "I love you so much," and other things that make you get teary-eyed
764. Luis!
765. When you left with purse in hand and came back with none
766. Knowing that it has to be somewhere between points AB and C but no idea where
767. Realizing that your car keys to your brand-new car were in said purse
778. Calling every place you were at and nobody seen nothing
779. (779) Screwing up the number system!

780. Calling all the locksmiths' place in the phonebook but none are open on Sunday
781. Getting your period at A and Q and you weren't prepared
782. Cramps
783. When little girl is named Daniel and then tell you her life history while you're peeing in a public restroom
784. Did I mention cramps?
785. Slamming your shin in between the crack and the closet door, getting a yucky-looking blister
786. Becoming your new roommate chauffeur because she can't drive
787. Having to make reservations for the Pufferbelly for nine people
788. Feeling sweaty
789. When your steering column smokes
790. When the interior lights in your car don't always work
791. When you haven't got a friend in Pennsylvania
792. When you're living in your parents' house and you don't have any privacy
793. When your stereo crackles
794. Waiting for something better to come along
795. When you can no longer get together with your friends and complain about anything and everything over a cup coffee
796. When you're living the life of a married forty-three years old, except you're twenty-one and single
797. When the best years of your life aren't and you've been looking forward to these years since you were twelve
798. When the best part of your day is when you fantasize that someday you're going to show your boss that you actually have intelligence and talent
799. When you see a wedding ring on the finger of one of your ex-boyfriends
800. Beaver Falls, Pennsylvania
801. The fact that you currently live there
802. When it's perfect camping weather but you have to go to work

803. Answering machines that cut you off
804. The double flusher when not all of it goes down the toilet the first time
805. Old people who try to dress like young people
806. Unnatural blondes
807. Unnatural blondes in pairs
808. The mall
809. That yucky stuff that collects on your tear ducts
810. People with '80s haircuts
811. That light and that light and that light and that light and that light
812. Your wallet being lost or getting stolen in Cleveland and having what you consider to be your whole life in it
813. Waiting to get your third new license in a year and you haven't gotten any DUIs
814. Sitting in a bar with a Diet Coke
815. Calling Russia and hearing "I love you" across the Atlantic when it's a bad connection
816. When your coffee cup shattered in a million pieces in Brady's and had been there for three years
817. Annoying flirtations come when you are obviously not remotely interested.
818. Forty-some-year-old deadhead teachers who try tongue action in the middle of the Nots.
819. Crying all of a sudden for what you feel is no reason because all of a sudden, your best friend gives you a hug, and you feel she's the only one who totally understood, and she's in Pennsylvania.
820. When you're worried about your sister's first night in a dorm room because she's not answering the phone and is probably doing everything you did but want to tell her not to do
821. Denny's
822. Feeling exhausted on the weekend
823. When you're worried about someone that you barely know but realize confronting her would almost force you to drudge up all your shitty past in one moment

824. Wanting to act like twelve and dress like you're sixteen, but you're twenty-one and feel old already
825. Having *no chalk* in college classroom on your first day teaching
826. Feeling fat but not wanting to work out
827. Having two good friends and wanting to help both, but they're on opposite sides
828. When a guy says, "It really hurts me to see you like this," and you get the feeling it only hurts him because it's not benefitting him
829. Sunday nights when you feel you just got up (you did)
830. When people say, "I'm still waiting for you to write a poem about __ and __, and you wish you could push a button and make one
831. Not being able to hear trains at night anymore
832. Losing a whole pack of cigarette
833. When your new driver's license and grad ID are one hundred times uglier than your previous one
834. Pain
835. Even worse, numbness
836. Flea bites
837. When your roommate's cat (Pepe) jumps on the counter and the stove after he's been outside all day, and you hit him like he's five, so he jumps down, but it doesn't do any good
838. When you have to eat standing up so your roommate's cat can't eat your microwave dinner
839. Microwave dinners
840. Bad puns and crappy jokes
841. When Janeen vibrantly describes her bodily functions, and you suddenly feel you, too, should use the bathroom
832. Finding that everything from #778 to # 841 is actually ten of where they should be, because whoever wrote # 769 got dyslexia
833. Not being able to suppress the urge to proofread everything
834. Me. (There, are you happy now?)
835. Self-deprecation

836. When people whom you care desperately about are really far away
837. Forgetting a word
838. #832 is grammatically incorrect
839. Promotions you don't really want
840. When people bitch at you for very petty things
841. Stains on the pages of TTS book
842. Driving all the way to Cleveland for two and half hours, having already lied to your workplace that you're sick, but you're really going for an interview and when you get there, they told you that they're on freeze and won't be hiring for a while
843. When someone whom you'd give the world for just acts like he wants to be friends
844. When the guy you like acts like friends when he's sober but wants to be more when he's been drinking
845. When you say the same thing twice in Janeen's book
846. Goodbyes (MER)
847. When your dog loves to empty your shoe closet when you're not around
848. Being single and the guy you like is staring you right in the face
849. People who go to the gym just walk in circles staring at you
850. Mike is leaving for Georgia for good
851. When people are late
852. When people make you wait
853. When it's your twenty-second birthday but it's "just another day in life"
854. When your adrenaline dies right after you've finished reading your poems
855. Lipstick on coffee cups
856. When A p'bgh poets hog the mic
857. When a P'bgh poet whom you know as acquaintance wants you to send him perfumed letters
858. The Amtrak passenger train has stopped running through Akron and Kent
859. One-way streets in Akron that you turn onto the wrong way

THINGS THAT SUCK

860. Term papers on word perfect
861. Peruvian delight
862. Holes in your muffler/tailpipe anyway, problems with your car when you only have plastic to pay for it
863. Seeing a student in Brady's and having a one-on-one conversation with him when it has nothing to do with class
864. Having a forty-some-year-old grimy-looking male tell you very drunkenly, "You're just too cute for your own good," over and over
865. Reading the Gyro bathroom wall where you wrote, "December 11, 1994, best night of my life," and then reading another woman's response: "September21, 1995, worst night of my life my love went away."
866. When your e-mail says, "0 messages," even though you've been mailing other people letters at least once a day
867. Losing a poem you don't have a copy of
868. When it's Homecoming weekend in Kent and there is tons of traffic.
869. Thinking about the last time you wrote in the TTS book
870. Looking out for everyone's asses
871. When you come home alone every night
872. When your roommate is vacuuming the carpet at 12:45 a.m.
873. Poets who read the same poem at every reading
874. Car commercials
875. People who have yet to come out of the '80s
876. My job
877. People who park their cars to blatantly block you in
878. Someone who doesn't know how to mind his own damn business
879. People who cause trouble just for the sake that they can
880. Karma
881. One day does not make a relationship?
882. Liars
883. When people bring things up that happened four years ago
884. Being scared
885. Flying out of Newark airport

886. Headaches
887. Trying to find a parking spot on the South side
888. Driving in Pittsburgh
889. Dishing out $800 when you don't have it
890. Taking your cat to be neutered
891. Working an hour and a half overtime and not being paid for it
892. Having to take money out of a CD
893. Morning headaches at one thirty
894. Your whole paycheck is going to government-like places
895. Commercialized Christmas
896. My job! My job My job My job My job My job My job My job My job My job My job!
897. Cold feet (Kitty's qualms)
898. Being stepped on
899. No more front claws
900. Drinking out of the bathroom sink and the faucet dripping on my head
901. Nobody will get up on Saturday to feed me
902. When my food is floating in my water dish
903. People who play with my chin
904. Hair balls in my throat
905. It's cold outside
906. Trying for a month to get together with an old friend, but the timing is always wrong
907. People who have laryngitis (sp?) but talk all the time just to remind you that they have laryngitis
908. Trying to spell laryngitis
909. Pittsburgh radio stations
910. Super narrow driveways that you scrape your wheels against every day
911. Chapped lips
912. No lip balm
913. When people tell you to take it with a grain of salt
914. When a good friend of yours tried to kill himself
915. Having said friend tell that you were part of the reason
916. The thermostat is up to seventy-five degrees and it's still cold

917. When your car battery dies at work in icy nasty weather
918. Leaving your car there overnight
919. Not knowing how you're going to get to work the next day
920. You were going to get AAA next month, too late now!
921. Salmon-flavored cream cheese
922. My job
923. Banana and garlic dressing
924. Being out of reefer, man
925. When your jaw feels like somebody put a clamp on it and attached it to tow truck that has already pulled it for two miles while you're sitting on the couch at home
926. When the "wax hand" has suddenly appeared in the medicine cabinet—it has a broken pinky, what next?
927. Having to lead an ordinary life when I don't have one
928. When you pour your milk into the cereal bowl and out of the carton comes big balls of fur like what you would expect a chunk of raccoon, that got peeled of the bone by a fifty series tire, to look like.
929. When you actually make it all the way to your car across an icy parking lot and just as you have the car door open—*wham!* You're on your butt.
930. When it's your employer's parking lot you fell on but you're not injured enough to sue them. The bastards!
931. Metropole on Saturday, JC.
932. Life without *the one true love* is all your love, JC
933. When people break their promises
934. The house is a mess
935. Not very good sex
936. The fact that it's now 1996
937. The more things change, the more they stay the same
938. The saying, "The more things change, the more they stay the same."
939. The cat's attitude
940. Mean people
941. Starting the new year off with clumsiness and hostility
942. Short shows

943. No encore
944. $128 phone bills
945. Buying meaningless things just to buy to cheer yourself up
946. Buying the wrong Christmas gift for someone and losing the receipt, so now you're stuck with it and have to spend more $ for the new correct gift
947. Spiders
948. Finding out the person mentioned in #348 has malaria and can't come back to the US 'til he's well
949. When the gas stove wasn't fully turned off and you come home and your whole place smells like gas
950. Knowing if you were gone a few more hours you could have killed your kitten
951. Withdrawal symptoms
952. Lunch isn't long enough
953. A sore throat
954. The beginning of being sick
955. A little bit of depression and a lot of wine do not make for having a very good time
956. Snow fucking, fucking snow!
957. The fact that my neighbors park their van at the top of the driveway, blocking the only access in and out of my own driveway
958. Winter
959. Shoveling snow
960. Not having enough time in a day to look for a new job
961. Dead palm trees
962. Not being in love
963. Wasting energy on being angry at nothing
964. Sharing a driveway
965. 6:14 a.m.
966. When your boss gives you one month to find a new job
967. Not seeing your best friend for three months
968. Job hunting
969. The idea of going through a temporary agency
970. The parking situation in Mt. Lebanon

971. Selfish neighbors
972. One week down, thee weeks to go and still no leads on a new job
973. Forgetting the "r" in three
974. Forgetting the "h" in three
975. Super bowl Sunday
976. Owing people money, yet you don't have any to give
977. Sore throats
978. Going out with a guy who is eleven years older
979. Taking a personal call in front of your boss
980. Leg stubble
981. Snow
982. Wondering where you are going to find the money you need to pay for everything you have to pay for
983. When your life is totally lame at its best
984. Having to do everything alone
985. Unhappiness
986. Defending your unhappiness to your mother
987. Missing Kent desperately
990. Having no friends where you live
991. Greener grass
992. Making three hundred cookies every week for the last two months
993. Being up at 12:28 still making cookies for this week
994. Old men who think that they're interested in a twenty-two-year-old girl
995. It's April, and yet winter lingers on.
996. Men who run out the door
997. Having an incredible night with a guy and never hearing from him again
998. Being a magnet for the divorced man
999. Not having Saturday off
1000. Knowing that in a little over a year, one thousand things have sucked
1001. State tax not withheld, $34
1002. Knowing that there has to be more to like than what you're currently doing

1003. The grammer mistake in #129
1004. Knowing on judgment day you and God are going to be talking for a very long time
1005. Not having written in TTS book since #873
1006. Twenty-nine total pages to write when your best friend's in Kent
1007. Visas (government ones)
1008. Waking up on the couch and some guy has his hand on your chest
1009. Crying like crazy and not at home
1010. Smartass college students who interrupt you every five seconds to tell you what you're doing wrong while you're teaching
1011. Racist outburst by some of your students—the vein in your neck is popping out—and you're trying to not show your own biases
1012. Spring and no one to share it with
1013. Taking $660 from your savings account because you want and have to anyway to live alone
1014. Knowing that the $660 only has taken you across the world and back
1015. Never feeling well rested
1016. Literary theory
1017. No ladybugs in this house (apartment)
1018. Reading this book over for the first time since #873
1019. The spelling error in #1003
1020. Students who guess your age to be twenty (wrong)
1021. Clocks ticking out of sync as you are trying to sleep
1022. Being taken advantage of
1023. Owing the city of Kent $18 and getting $9 back. Nine dollars back from the state of Ohio
1024. The state of Ohio
1025. #1000, because way more than one thousand things sucked last year, don't you think?
1026. Getting used to "Janeen in Kent" and then she has to go to Pennsylvania again
1027. No parking in downtown Kent

1028. Scrubbing mildew off the bathtub
1029. Listening to Sandra whine
1030. Ten and a half months without him
1031. Thirteen and a half until he can come back
1032. Reading things he wrote here
1033. When Luis always walks past your place but never stops and then calls to say he saw your car and it always feels like he's spying on you
1034. This girl Heather with the nasal voice
1035. There are never any phone calls for me!
1036. Finding a summer job
1037. When your students finally figure out you're only getting your master's, not a PhD, and oh, you aren't even a part-timer.
1038. Credit cards that expire this month
1039. Emphysema
1040. Smoking like a chimney when you know your grandma is dying of #1039
1041. Two days ago, you check your checking account, and it's over $1000 and tonight it says $224.
1042. Dribble
1044. Thinking you had enough handwritten pages and obtained three typewritten ones but you ended up with one and a half
1045. Drinking wine on a Sunday night when you have a lot to do tomorrow
1046. The candles that went out at May fourth memorial
1047. Getting addicted to computers
1048. Sleeping on the couch when you know the cat thinks it's his bed, not yours
1049. Burps
1050. The fact that you should be treating your friend because she's a guest but she treats you instead because you're perpetually poor
1051. The fact that said friend is a guest
1052. Not being able to smoke inside your place
1053. Getting your second wind but not wanting to finish the paper until tomorrow at the last minute

1054. Bar stamps
1055. Chipped nail polish
1056. Neen's jeans that you kissed Konnie in for the first time
1057. Ripped pages
1058. When the strap (shoulder) on your bag breaks, and consequently you carry it with the hand-straps, and your back aches constantly
1059. Finals week
1060. Students who want to know their grades every other day
1061. Presentations on psychoanalytic feminism
1062. Having to go to campus when you don't want to
1063. Rancid French dressing all over the back seat in your car
1064. Trying to do what's best
1065. Making a good friend leave
1066. When memories plague you
1067. Regretting what you have done and who you've been with in the past
1068. Hoping and praying that it doesn't affect your future
1069. Car insurance rates
1070. A big fat ten cents raise
1071. Watching someone very close to you go through surgery
1072. Having the police call all the time for your ex-roomate
1073. Spelling *roommate* wrong
1074. Money matters
1075. My boss's attitude
1076. When your boss accuses you of something she did
1077. Not having the person you love around to share a glass of wine with
1078. #51
1079. #76
1080. #80
1081. Wondering if you'll graduate
1082. #92
1083. meant to say #91
1084. #101. Reading #101 now
1085. #113

1086. #137 and seeing said professor before class starts anyhow
1087. #139
1088. Using old entries for things that suck instead of saying something original
1089. Seeing Janeen for the first time since September
1090. Doing a thesis
1091. Getting lost in Pennsylvania when we were so close to arriving
1092. Stress that affects your body
1093. Blood tests and no one knows what's wrong
1094. Mushy poems by guys all the time
1095. Living alone
1096. Leaky ceiling
1097. Moving again
1098. No job and an MA at twenty-three
1099. Will I get an MA in May?
2000. Comprehensive exams
2001. Coupons with an expiration date of 1/1/01
2002. Knowing you should go to sleep but can't
2003. Hairy legs
2004. Quitting smoking
2005. Making mistakes while teaching and feeling paranoid that your students are laughing at you
2006. The ex-students who come to see you every Thursday without fail
2007. Pinched nerves
2008. Computers
2009. Misprinting something on a final copy
2010. Wimpy thesis advisors
2011. Never going out
2012. Ugly fingernails when they used to be long
2013. Not getting letter of recommendation in time to apply for a great job
2014. Your parents' twenty-fifth wedding anniversary and you have no clue what to get them, and even if you did, you would have any money to get something nice
2015. No one to cry with

2016. Sleeping with someone in your bed and feeling alone
2017. Knowing I could fill twenty lines without really having to think
2018. Regretted tattoos
2019. Teething
2020. Working every weekend
2021. Jeans that make you look fat and bras that make you look flat
2022. Pantyhose
2023. Putting your underwear on inside out and not realizing it for hours
2024. Getting a dream job offer and your husband doesn't want you to take the job
2025. 2011 and 2012
2026. Pantyhose again!
2027. Migraines
2028. Look at the sixth page
2029. Trying to find a new job
2030. Moving twice within one year
2031. Moving ten days before Christmas
2032. When you're not in the Christmas spirit
2033. Freaking out on the people who love you the most
2034. Idiocy
2035. When you've told your ex-boyfriend that you're married now, and he goes and writes a heartfelt letter about how sorry he is that he hurt you during your relationship with him
2036. Fish with ice
2037. Fish with birth defects
2038. Pimples at age twenty-four; new kittens qualms
2039. Not being able to scratch the carpet and furniture
2040. The other cat hogs both food dishes
2041. Getting really dizzy when someone throws me up in the air and spins me like a helicopter
2042. Falling down the stairs
2043. Running after the peacock feather and bumping into the table
2044. People who park in your parking spot
2045. Being the only employee

2046. Bangs that hang in your eyes
2047. The fact that we call hair on your forehead bangs
2048. Forgetting to do things
2049. Bronchial Infections
2050. Human beings who walk the earth all their lives without clue!
2051. When you can't remember the date of someone's birthday but you know too well to ask them
2052. Realizing that you are one of the people described in #2050
2053. Grumpy old men who probably haven't smiled in the last twenty years
2054. The MAC machine
2055. Utilities
2056. Trying to find a house for 75k or under
2057. The movie *Hairspray*
2058. Not having any scotch tape
2059. Cold feet
2060. When your hubby keeps the house around fifty-two degrees Fahrenheit
2061. Commercials
2062. Columbine High shootings
2063. Really cheesy TV shows
2064. Miracle whip with a sale by date of October '98 and it's now June '99
2065. People who can't follow rules
2066. People who are in a hurry
2067. Remembering the meeting you were supposed to go to three days late
2068. Cookies that fall apart when you bite into them
2069. Wrinkled shirts
2070. Spillage
2071. Long, wrinkled, long stupid RU shirts
2072. Lost checks
2073. Being interrupted in the middle of something important
2074. The grammar mistake in #998
2075. Working on Friday and Saturday and not being able to see your girlfriend for a month

2076. Mary Marburger
2077. Getting screwed
2078. Slow computers
2079. Bad days
2080. The penalty box
2081. Big huge hairy moths
2082. Not having any food in the house
2083. When the air conditioning conks out at the drive-in box (16x7)!
2093. No air suffocating!
2094. People who think that the world owes them something
2095. When the "brake" light keeps coming on when you're driving
2096. People who are "old" at heart
2097. Tense situations
2098. Forgetting to send a card until one day before an occasion so the card won't get there 'til after the occasion
3000. Being #3000 and not written since # 2014, which was two years ago
3001. Joplin, Missouri
3002. Being in the middle of two great friends who are sexually involved secretly with each other
3003. Not being able to handle drinking more than a few beers anymore
3004. Wretched hangovers
3005. Reading old entries and wondering who the hell I was just four years ago
3006. Overly zealous religious fanatic students
3007. Taking three half weeks to read a book in Spanish (for the first in a good year)
3008. Arthritic dogs
3009. Having a gay partner at a wedding
3010. Not hooking up with anyone at a wedding
3011. When no one notices anything different about you
3012. Summer 1999 heat wave
3013. The spots where the words have faded or been erased in this book

3014. Rejection letters
3015. Regretting things
3016. Falling asleep early
3017. Wanting and needing to use the bathroom but not wanting to wake people up
3018. Being inside an old house that's arranged differently on the inside than the way you had it, thus, confusing your memory of the way it had been
3019. Slumping baseball teams
3020. Flea bites
3021. Not having washed off your makeup from the night before and realizing you've left a nice all-mascara stain on the pillowcase
3022. Buying and trying on jeans
3023. Bad morning breath
3024. Range Line Road in Joplin, Missouri
3025. Hicks with bumper stickers for the right to carry (arms)
3026. Dreams you can only remember the very edges of
3027. Worrying about tornado living in Missouri
3028. People who call Missouri "Missourah"
3029. Bananas
3030. Dirty-looking fingernails
3031. When you want to get the teeth whitening thing done and it's $350
3032. Time
3033. Doctoral applications
3034. The GRE when you never had to take it for an MA but need to now
3035. It's been how many years since you had math? You did *how* in math?
3036. Eating something you don't like just because it'd be rude not to
3037. Having to return a rental car early Monday instead of hanging out longer here
3038. Having your mail held for a month, which will make your bills late, and you have to pay extra
3039. Buzzing noise

3040. Cooking for one—if it's good, only you know; if it's bad, you eat cheese-its for dinner
3041. Coming home after a really long day and no one is there, and there are no messages and no recent mail
3042. "Junk" e-mail messages
3043. Neighbors of your parents' being way too concerned with your love life—or lack thereof
3044. Gas
3045. Having to write #3044. (Gross)
3046. Friends that ditch you because they're dating someone new
3046. When the new someone is so not worth it, but "who are you to judge?"
3047. Not having answered an eighteen-page letter you received in March (now July) in which a male friend addressed his undying affection for you
3048. Wanting to answer the letter but not knowing what to say and how
3049. When said person has no clue what he's talking about
3050. Zits at age twenty-five
3051. The fact that I am twenty-five
3052. Not knowing what you want or whom you want
3053. Chasing after the same guy for over a year and half to no avail
3054. Chasing after a guy when you like it the other way
3055. When people say not to analyze much but you're a Virgo and can't help it
3056. Counting on a little horoscope boost, though you say how stupid horoscopes are
3057. Putting empty cereal boxes, milk jugs, etc. back with only a spoonful left
3058. Mosquito-spraying truck smell and sound
3059. Cristobal
3060. Faculty meetings lasting longer than half hour
3061. Meetings on Fridays
3062. No coffee shops in all of Joplin, Missouri.
3063. Not sleeping when I should
3064. Inflamed Gluteal Muscles

THINGS THAT SUCK

3065. Those dammed "problem days"
3066. Labeling as 2,000 something instead of 3,000
3067. High gas prices
3068. Finally having a relationship again but realizing you need to end it
3069. The fact I'm twenty-six.
3070. Over explaining poems
3071. Having to communicate through writing when you want to talk
3072. Mentioning "toxic waste" in two separate poems by two different people
3073. When your boob falls out of your bra
3074. People who walk reeealllly sssllloooowwwlllyyy
3075. realizing #3074 is really hard to read
3076. Computers that don't want to do what you tell them to
3077. Creating a great document on your computer and losing the file
3078. Wasting a day by not getting anything good accomplished!
3079. Not enough hours in a day
3080. Getting nervous!
3081. Snow
3082. When you try to call someone and they are on the Internet forever!
3083. Having to pee but holding it because you have other things you have to do
3084. The computers here!
3085. Having to answer for someone else
3086. Everything is a priority
3087. Trying to juggle work and home life and feeling guilty on both sides
3088. Allergies
3089. One-minute loans!
3090. Stupid files that are two big and freeze up even when you try to do something as simple as scroll down
3091. Cramps in the arch of your foot that won't go away even after three days

3092. When the radio plays the same three songs over and over again
3093. Boys
3094. When you're halfway through a project and your boss tells you to do it differently and you have to do it all over again
3095. That chocolate is not a healthy food
3096. Gaining fifteen pounds and having to buy all new clothes
3097. Cottage cheese thighs
3098. Boys who point out that I have cottage cheese thighs
3099. Safe deposit boxes
3100. Being single
3101. Matthew Levengood
3102. Our new PCs
3103. Idiots that think you can learn a new system out of a book
3104. Boys that say they're going to call and never do
3105. Copier machines that jam
3106. Brown pens
3107. Being on time and then bad things happen and now you're behind
3108. #705, #334, #335, and heroine
3109. Bitchiness!
3110. The fact that the page with #3056 through #3091 is falling out and must be taped!
3111. When your printer disappears from your computer
3112. The fact that there are only two pages left to write in the TTS book
3113. You try and try but you can't do anything right all the way down to how your keys are on your key chain
3114. Unconstructive criticism
3115. Knowing you should just give up "trying to please" and knowing that you'll just keep trying
3116. Constantly trying to run through that "brick wall."
3117. When people take you too literally and you're making a joke and they are so "know it all" that they actually correct your sarcasm
3118. #38, #39, #40, and #51 smeared
3119. People who are too serious!

3120. The realization that you're just not special anymore
3121. The "anymore" on the above statement assumes that you were at one time and now you're thinking it was all in your head
3122. These cotton pick "in" instructor's notes!
3123. A husband who can't make his own doctor's appointment and he has to call his "mommy" to do it for him
3124. Broken car doors
3125. Forty-some-year-olds who act they're twelve (particularly women)
3126. People who spend money on dumb things and then bitch that they will be poor their entire lives
3127. When your mother needs to call you every day
3128. When your mother gets hurt when you tell her not to call so often
3129. Having a long-distance relationship again, especially when you're unsure if it's worth it
3130. Heavy drinkers
3131. People who drink your booze act like they didn't know what they were doing (sneaking booze)
3132. Not being able to tell #31 how you feel for nearly two years
3133. Regretting sex
3134. Worrying about birth control
3135. Worrying about sex
3136. Guilt
3137. A friend your age who's getting divorced after two years of marriage
3138. Back seat drivers
3139. The puny "cars" on the way to the The Arch
3140. Not that guy!
3141. The way you eat when your chef-boyfriend isn't around
3142. Chewing on/biting the inside of your mouth (your dad always said it'd give you cancer)
3143. Getting on the Internet and staying online mindlessly for hours
3144. People who talk over your head to hear themselves talk
3145. Zits. Again. This time at twenty-seven and on your lip!

3146. Seeing a cute boy wanting to flirt, even though you're in a relationship
3147. Social butterfly boys
3148. Realizing you are not a teacher anymore but one of those kinds of students you always hated, the kind who stay after class to ask questions
3149. The yucky outside of your apartment building
3150. Annoying entertainment news programs
3151. Saying "I'm sorry" all the time even when you have nothing to be sorry for
3152. The end of this book—I just can't believe it!
3153. Moths
3154. Killing moths
3155. The price of flowers
3156. Anyone who murders, and especially anyone who murders children
3157. Car alarms going off
3158. Bass in car stereos so loud you'd think the glass might break. *Why?*
3159. Does the aged look of TTS book reflect the age of its two primary writers?
3160. Having a student removed from your class for sexual harassment
3161. Having your boss question one of your colleagues behind your back about whether it was "really so bad" after he'd just told you to your face, "This is obviously a case of sexual harassment."
3162. Living in an apartment below your landlord in a house he's been there since 1965 (305 N. Connor Avenue, Joplin)
3163. Having your AC on continually because it's so hot in St. Louis
3164. Your electric bill that hasn't arrived yet with all that AC time on it
3165. Having to shave your bikini line
3166. Growing your hair long again
3167. PMS boobs (sorry, I know. Gross)

3168. People who think they're "cool" because they wear name brands. Come on, folks, it ain't the '80s
3179. When the live band's so loud you can't hear the other person talk
3180. Irritable bowel syndrome (IBS alias)
3181. Fake Mozzarella (sp?)
3182. Musicians doing covers all night long
3183. Four days isn't long enough
3184. Realizing you sound like your mom when you said you never would
3185. Ditto
3186. Constantly, with everything, finding something to regret—"I should have"
3187. Feeling bloated, like your stomach has a basketball in it, before you go to sleep, well, anytime, but especially before you want to sleep
3188. Bars that have the nerve to charge money just for the "privilege" of entrance
3189. When an experience takes you back in time and you wonder if you could have built a whole different life for yourself
3190. Remembering a time when you were complete
3191. Saying out loud, "I'm unhappy!"
3192. Understanding a time in your life is past and feeling it just may be the happiest time ever
3193. It's the last line of the first thing in the TTS book.

And thus the search for the *Things That Suck* Book II begins September 1, 2001, Saturday.

CPSIA information can be obtained
at www.ICGtesting.com
Printed in the USA
BVHW032318140119
537850BV00001B/66/P